The Little Mern

illustrated by Laura Barella

Child's Play (International) Ltd
Ashworth Rd, Bridgemead, Swindon, SN5 7YD UK
Swindon   Auburn ME   Sydney
© 2012 Child's Play (International) Ltd   Printed in Heshan, China
ISBN 978-1-84643-443-3   L021111CFT12114433
1 3 5 7 9 10 8 6 4 2
www.childs-play.com

There was once a little mermaid, who lived
at the bottom of the sea with her older sisters.
They spent many happy hours playing with the
nimble creatures of the deep. The little mermaid
was the fastest swimmer of them all!

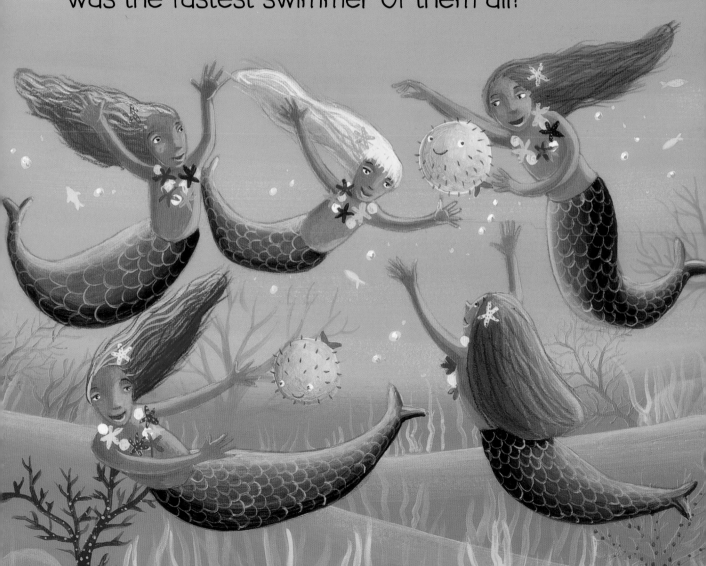

One day, the little mermaid saw one
of her sisters swimming down from above.
"What's up there?" she asked.
"That's the surface," answered her sister.
"I've been watching the humans! One day you will
be old enough to go up there and see for yourself."

Sure enough, the day came when the little mermaid was allowed to go to the surface. "It's so much lighter than home," she thought excitedly. "But the air is so dry!"

She was just about to swim back down
to her beloved ocean deep, when a ship came
wallowing into view. She could see humans
running around on its decks.
"They look so funny," she thought.
"Ocean creatures are much more graceful!"

All of a sudden,
a storm blew up.

The ship leaned over,
and one of the humans
fell into the water.

The little mermaid swam
towards him slowly. He was
splashing and gasping so much
that she thought he must be
playing. She laughed, delighted
to have found a playmate.

But when she got nearer, she saw that he was scared. Because he didn't have a tail, swimming was very difficult for him, and he could not breathe when his face was under the water. Soon, he seemed to go to sleep, and something told her to swim to him and keep him afloat in her arms.

They drifted with the waves, until it was calm.
They floated close to a sandy beach, and the little
mermaid dragged the sleeping boy up onto the hot
dry sand. She watched the beach from the sea,
to make sure he came to no more harm.

After a while, a woman came along the sand.
She woke the boy, and helped him walk up the
beach to a large white palace. The little mermaid
breathed a sigh of relief, and swam away.

In the days that followed, the little mermaid often swam near the beach to watch the boy. She was fascinated by the land, by the hot, bright sun, the dusty sand and the mountains in the distance. She longed to find out more about this world, so different from her own.

Her sisters wondered what was going on.
"You never play with us any more," they
complained. "Where do you go every day?"
"To the surface," she explained.
"I'd love to live on land."

"Don't be silly," they laughed.
"You belong here with us!
You'd hate it up there."
"I'll show you!" she replied.
"I'll go and live with the humans!"

The next morning, the little mermaid swam
nervously to the cave of the sea witch.

"I see," said the witch. "If you want to spend time
on land, a tail is no good. I can give you a pair of
legs, but beware! If you ever change your mind,
I will not be able to give you back your tail."
"My mind is made up," answered the little mermaid.
"Please work your magic."

In an instant, she felt a strange feeling in her tail.
When she looked down, she saw a pair of legs
instead! They felt very odd, and it took her
ages to swim to the beach.

She dragged herself onto the sand, and stood up slowly. The air was hot and dry. As she began to hobble painfully away from her beloved ocean, the boy she had saved came along the beach. "Hello!" he said. "Have you been for a swim?"

They walked along the beach, and became the firmest friends. The boy showed her the biggest rock pools, his secret cave and the best place to climb the cliffs. He showed her the mountains of his kingdom, the lakes and the waterfalls. They watched the sun rise and the moon set.

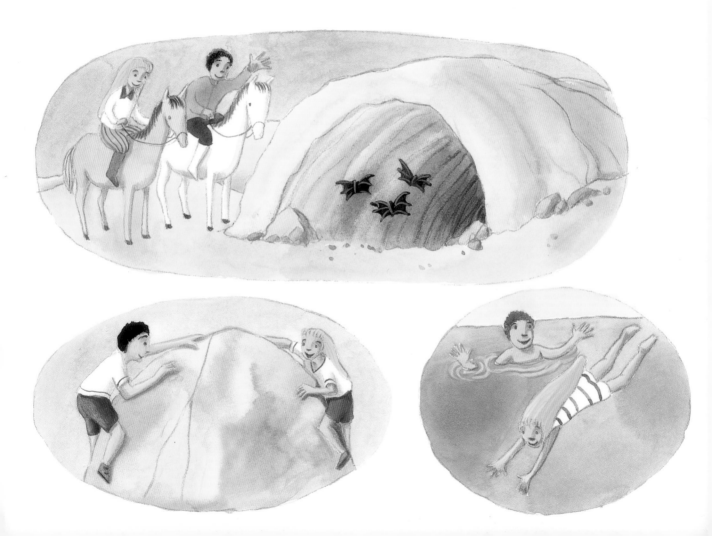

The boy showed her the palace where he lived. "I'm a prince," he explained. "I'm supposed to be important. I'm not allowed to do anything for myself."

At first, the little mermaid
was excited by this new
world, but as the days went
by, she began to miss
her ocean home.

The bright sun was too hot, and the air too dry.
She missed her sisters, the cool waters of the depths,
and the many creatures of the sea. Her legs ached
and she felt slow and clumsy. She remembered
how gracefully she had once been able to swim.

One night, she left the prince a farewell note. She crept silently from the palace down to the beach. Under the silver moonlight, she walked slowly into the water. Then, with tears in her eyes, she slid beneath the surface of the waves.

As she swam, the little mermaid realized how much she had missed her old home. Her family welcomed her back with open arms. Bit by bit, she began to enjoy the ocean once again. As before, she played happily with her sisters and the sea creatures.

But she was no longer the fastest swimmer of them all. Swimming with her legs was much harder than with her powerful tail.

From time to time, the little mermaid feels a little lonely. She swims slowly to the surface of the sea to sit quietly, looking towards land. And every now and again, the prince can be seen walking by himself along the beach beside a white palace, and sometimes he will stop and gaze quietly out to sea.